THE GENETIC PRESCRIPTION

Book 2 - Healing your DNA with Genetic Oil Elixirs™

ELYCE MONET

ISBN 978-1-957943-69-5 (paperback)
ISBN 978-1-957943-70-1 (digital)

The author of this book does not dispense medical advice or prescribe the use of any technique as a form of treatment for physical, emotional, or medical problems without the advice of a physician, either directly or indirectly. The intent of the author is only to offer information of a general nature to help you in your quest for emotional and spiritual well-being. In the event you use any of the information in this book for yourself, which is your constitutional right, the author and the publisher assume no responsibility for your actions.

Any people depicted in stock imagery provided by Thinkstock are models, and such images are being used for illustrative purposes only.
Certain stock imagery © Thinkstock.

Rushmore Press LLC
1 800 460 9188
www.rushmorepress.com

Printed in the United States of America

This book is dedicated to anyone
searching for hope and healing.

*Physicists have discovered that your genetic codes (DNA)
respond to both your inner and outer environments. By
properly using Genetic Oil Elixirs™, and finding the source
of old belief systems, habits and patterns, your awareness can
catalyze the DNA codes within you. The result is that your
health and your life will be improved in your outer reality.
It is the Universal principle of "As within-So without".*

*This book is a manual for anyone who wants to catalyze
their DNA and bring it to a higher level in order to
experience better health, peace, happiness and love.*

"We are not victims of our genes, but masters of our fates, able
to create lives overflowing with peace, happiness, and love."

— Bruce H. Lipton, <u>The Biology of Belief: Unleashing
the Power of Consciousness, Matter and Miracles</u>

CONTENTS

ABOUT THE AUTHOR

Elyce Monet is a spiritual healer and wisdom teacher who healed herself after three near-death experiences. She has been on a spiritual journey for more than 30 years. She conducts private sessions and workshops to assist people to heal from the inside out.

Her first book, "The Yeshua Prescription", taught healing in a non-traditional way, combining biblical formulas and principles used by Yeshua and the Essenes for plant-based preparations for healing. She has upgraded those formulas and has added crystalline energies from crystals that have been known for thousands of years to expedite and magnify healing.

This book is an extension of her original work, written for all faiths, cultures and peoples. It provides an understanding of taking control of your destiny and clearing your DNA of ancestral patterns and stuck energies within your body. It will impact the frequency of your DNA and improve your capacity to heal. The methodologies combine centuries of knowledge about DNA from science, philosophy from the iChing, and teachings by Master Teachers of Light.

ABOUT THE FORMULATORS

 **Elyce Monet** is working together with the spiritual Masters (including Larry Secor who passed on in 2021) and Cathy Chapman to create new formulations that include crystalline frequencies. She is delighted to bring forth an even higher vibration to a new line of oils.

 **Cathy Chapman, PhD.** is working with Elyce and Larry to create a line of Elixir Oils. Her background includes a PhD in mind-body-spirit medicine and essential oils. She has been treating and healing patients for several decades, and was also friends with Larry Secor.

 **Larry Secor** formulated the first line of healing oils for Elyce Monet's first book, "The Yeshua Prescription". Our new line includes the use of those formulas, along with crystalline elixirs to add higher vibrational energies for additional healing. It is written in fond memory of Larry, who passed in 2021.

ABOUT THIS BOOK

When I published my first book, "The Yeshua Prescription" it was targeted toward Christians to help them understand the healing power of plant medicine, just as Yeshua taught his disciples. It became very clear that the larger group of people who are interested in mind-body-spirit medicine needed a book and a formula that is updated to include not only the biblical oil formulas, but crystalline energies, with light and prayer added to the mix to create an even higher vibration to catalyze healing of DNA.

Since Covid-19, it has become clear that my information received prior to my last book, about the plagues and end times, has arrived. My friend, Larry Secor, passed on, and still sends me his love, his light and his encouragement to go beyond what we did together. Thus, the writing of this book and the creation of new oil formulas.

We need to learn how to heal our bodies as naturally as possible, instead of taking chemical preparations when they are unnecessary. Our society has unfortunately trained us to "take a pill" to heal whatever ails us. It's a habit we need to break if we are going to heal on all levels.

I am a firm believer that all disease (dis-ease) in the body comes first through the spiritual realm through 33 different dimensions around our bodies. Some call it the "Adam Kadmon" and it has been written about in many books about higher vibrational man, including "The Keys of Enoch" and "The Melchizadek Method". When it finally gets to the physical, we have lots of work to do to identify the mental, emotional, physical and spiritual habits and patterns that allowed it to get that far. But there is hope! **We have all the things we need.** It is usually our attitudes, habits and patterns that need attention. Once we address the root cause of our illness through the dimensions, we can clear it. It's not as hard as it sounds! And this book is written to guide you into total self-honesty and healing as a master of your own fate.

Take your time! Healing doesn't necessarily come quickly, although sometimes it does. Remember, it took you years to manifest the dis-ease in your physical body. Our oil elixirs will open your mind, body, emotions and spirit to find the shadows that can be healed within you. Your genetics are designed to be healed and your frequencies in your DNA elevated. You simply need to find the genes that are not yet "turned on" in the light. It sometimes takes a guide who can look at your body inter-dimensionally and understand what is going on. Both my partner, Cathy Chapman, and I are trained to do that and can guide you if you desire. Simply email me at elyce@ elycemonet.com. Even without a guide, you can begin your healing with Genetic Healing Oil Elixirs™ on your own with this book, and that's a great place to start.

INTRODUCTION TO HEALING WITH GENETIC OIL ELIXIRS™

This book is a manual for healing your DNA through prayer, meditation and anointing with Genetic Oil Elixirs™. It is designed to provide you with an effective way of healing yourself spiritually, emotionally, mentally and physically. They are not intended to take the place of any medical advice or treatment, but can be used practically and safely for healing as an adjunct therapy to any medical treatment safely.

Our oils are formulated with all-natural ingredients (no toxic ingredients or additives) and the healing power of the vibration (the WORD) of Creator's voice during creation and the crystalline energy from specific crystals that were created to be used as healing frequencies. Genetic Healing Oil Elixirs™ contain the very essence of creation, combining both plant- based oils and crystalline elixirs.

Please note that it is not just the oil elixirs that bring healing. Your spiritual, emotional, mental and physical states, as well as your belief systems, attitudes, habits and patterns, have everything to do with whether or not you heal.

As you progress with the healing methodologies in this manual, you may bump up against something that will challenge the way you have thought about yourself; your beliefs, and how you approached healing in the past. Agree to be challenged! If a belief system is ready to be let go, let it go so you can heal! Try all the healing prayers and meditations contained in this book. When I was near death, I decided that I was willing to do anything to heal, even if it meant having to stand on my head naked in the corner! While that seems like a silly statement, that is how surrendered to we need to be when it comes to healing. I felt no shame or condemnation over trying it all, and I wasn't worried about what anybody else thought. I was simply on a mission to learn what had caused my illness and how I could change it so I could heal. I stood before my Creator naked, with nothing to hide. Healing begins when we are able to be completely **transparent**. No secrets! No denial! We must be willing to come to Creator warts and all!

I knew that my time of service here on planet Earth was not complete, so I needed to do my due diligence to find out what I had done to cause this and how I could heal myself. Remember, Creator uses all things in our lives to get us to understand our oneness and how all is connected. Even our illnesses are used to bring us to a state of understanding our mistakes as co-creators.

We are co-creators with Source, which gives us an enormous responsibility to look at our part in the creation of our own illness and disease. If we can understand and humble ourselves enough to understand the trauma or decisions that created the initial root of illness, we can heal ourselves. We can learn much about ourselves if we are willing to open our eyes, ears and hearts and be willing to face the truth and take responsibility for ourselves. We have been taught that Creator is outside of us, but the truth is that Creator is within us. Every cell in our bodies has the imprint of Creator. It's time we began operating like we are co-creators rather than victims of our suffering. The keys lie within our DNA codes, and they can be turned on by our intention, focus, prayer, meditation and cleansing.

I found in my ongoing pursuit for healing, that belief systems are the primary key to whether or not we heal. What is a belief system? It is simply something we think and feel repetitively until it becomes embodied, and we act on it subconsciously as truth. Most times, these are old belief systems we took on from the conditioning of our parents and authority figures while growing up and the feelings surrounding them. We need to examine them for truth and let them go if they no longer resonate with where we are. Let me give you an example of a very prominent belief system that gets in the way of our healing.

We have been conditioned to believe that healing is external and always physical in nature. Often, when we get sick, we take a pill or have something (like an organ) cut out. The problem with that kind of belief system is that it never addresses the underlying cause of the illness; it simply cuts out the organ. How many other organs will be affected if we don't get to the root of the problem? Traditional medical doctors have unfortunately been trained in this belief system, adhering to only chemical compound prescriptions and surgery as the answer in the physical realm. In fact, it is written in their Scope of Practice by the American Medical Association! They can't do it another way (alternatively) without getting in trouble with the licensing board. Most times they end up treating symptoms rather than identifying the source of the manifestation of illness in the body.

In order to look deeper into the causes of dis-ease in the body, it takes an open heart to listen to and try new therapies, whether they are covered by insurance or not! As I have worked with many, I have found that often the limiting belief has been around money. "I can't afford it" is often the most common block to healing. While our society has been conditioned to go to doctors and hospitals that cost thousands of dollars, it is easy to set up that mental block. The truth, however, is that you can make great strides in your health by changing that belief system and opening up to the infinite supply of abundance as a co-creator!

I remember in my own life saying I could never afford my healing. My doctor at the time reminded me that if I put myself first and let the universe supply what I needed, I would create an environment for myself that was conducive to my healing and money wouldn't be a problem. That year I worked half as hard and tripled my income. My expenses were covered. I began to see that I had the power to co-create my life the way I wanted it to be, and that included money and health.

Because our minds and belief systems are so powerful, we are very often completely unaware of what we are doing that is not in alignment with Universal Truth (creator within us) until it's too late and illness manifests. That's when we need to accept that we have been asleep at the wheel. But don't despair! You got yourself into this, and you can get yourself out! It will take perseverance and patience, but you can do it! Your self awareness and ownership of your own part in your disease is the first step to healing it!

It is believed by many doctors now who study epigenetics and human biology, that the real reason we get sick is because we are repeatedly experiencing traumas on many different levels that are repressed and ignored. This is all caused by our lack of understanding and awareness. It is easy for us to see "stress" as a trigger and a cause, but how do we pinpoint what "stress" is? How do we understand the differences between mental stress, emotional stress, environmental stress, ancestral stress, physical stress, etc.? It is high time we get to the roots of illness so they can be cleansed once and for all, rather than going to a doctor for treatment of symptoms. We need to learn that all healing happens within us on a cellular level. When you work with your open mind and heart, beyond the limits of human belief systems, miracles can happen within your cells! I am living proof. I have healed myself when diagnosed as near death three times.

We need to learn to be patient with ourselves. It is like peeling the layers of an onion. It takes work. It can make you cry. It takes insight. It takes surrender like you've never surrendered before, layer by layer. Through the journey, however, you will find out many beautiful things about yourself. You will learn how precious you are, and that you have enormous power within you to heal and change your life for the better. Everything in our lives, including illness, is there to help us come to terms with how to switch on our genetics to a higher frequency that changes the cellular structure and eliminates illness.

I also personally recommend ALL HEALING MODALITIES, so as not to limit healing. Our bodies are very complicated, and can and should be treated simultaneously medically, holistically, and spiritually. This manual is a guide to help you heal traumas primarily from a spiritual perspective (because it involves mind-body-spirit), but we do not believe that oils and spiritual practices are the ONLY way to heal. If you are sick, get help from all sources you trust. I traveled the world working on my health with many Masters in Eastern Medicine as well as working with traditional Medical Doctors and Natural Holistic Practitioners. They all have a place in our healing, as do prescription drugs.

If I have an infection in my body, it is prudent to get an antibiotic to clear the infection. If I have a broken leg, I want a medical doctor to reset it, not a spiritual healer (although I reset my own broken hand beautifully with faith without knowing it was broken!) I personally utilize as many holistic practices as possible, because I believe the more natural the better. However, use your own inner guidance to guide you to what feels right and wrong. You are the one in the driver's seat of your ongoing healing, not any doctor, healer, family member or friend. You know your body and soul better than anyone except Creator. Go within yourself to ask Creator what your steps are to co-create great health. You might be surprised. You may get guidance to go to a therapist that can help you heal your emotional wounds. You might be guided to get acupuncture to release stuck energy. You might be guided to exercise and diet. You might be guided to get significant blood panels to discover bacteria and viruses that may be in your body. And you might be guided to work on ancestral issues lying dormant in your DNA.

Healing is all done in stages. We all have more than just the physical body. We are multi-dimensional beings, and for healing to work, we need to work on all the subtle bodies (emotional, mental, spiritual, etc.) as well as the physical. Let your heart guide you step by step. Listen to everyone, and make your decisions in your prayer closet, alone with your higher self. When your heart is flooded with peace, you will know you are on the right path.

THE HISTORY OF HEALING OILS

S acred healing oils have been used in healing practices and ceremonies for thousands of years, and are still prominent today as non-toxic, medicinal remedies. Our oils have been extracted from plant essences and formulated from both Biblical references and the study of the teachings of Jesus Christ and the Essenes, the healing group from which we believe Him to have belonged and practiced.

The Essenes were the healers of their time. Dr. Edmond Bordeaux Szekely, a principal translator of Essene materials before the discovery of the Dead Sea Scrolls, describes the Essene Community:

"They spent much time in study, both of ancient writings and special branches of learning, such as education, healing and astronomy In the use of plants and herbs for healing man and beast they were likewise proficient.

They lived a simple regular life, rising each day before sunrise to study and commune with the forces of nature, bathing in cold water as a ritual and donning white garments. After their daily labor in the fields and vineyards they partook of their meals in silence, preceding and ending it with prayer. They were entirely vegetarian in their eating and never touched flesh foods nor fermented liquids. Their evenings were devoted to study and communion with the heavenly forces. ...

Their way of life enabled them to live to advanced ages of 120 years or more and they were said to have marvelous strength and endurance. In all their activities they expressed creative love."

This manual is designed to provide you with simple first steps to learn the same healing methods Jesus Christ practiced while he was on Earth. You have everything you need within you to open your heart and heal yourself, as long as you are within Divine will. The oils, prayers and sacred ceremonies are simply suggestions and tools for connecting you to the Christ, His holy angels, and other enlightened Masters. Your work, which will be outlined in this manual, will be to learn how to **receive** the Divine Essences and the emanations of the Holy Spirit and the living vibration of Creator contained in your Genetic Healing Oil Elixirs™.

Healing is an ongoing process which requires minute by minute self-examination, prayer, meditation and action. We are exhorted to take every thought captive for the uplifting of all, and I have found that our thoughts are the very key to overcoming disease. Our minds are so powerful that we can actually override our natural intuition, which is our Divine Guidance system. Whatever your first intuition is about something, learn how to trust it! It is usually the right answer for you! Once you start analyzing things, your mind takes over, and you become the victim of the imprints of the authorities in your life while growing up, which may or may not be truth. We learn as children from the imprints of our parents, teachers, and other authority figures, and those imprints are embedded in our subconscious minds. We don't even know they are influencing us, but they are! The secret is to re-learn to trust our intuition. Your intuition and listening to your inner guidance provides you with many secrets to healing yourself. You are your own healer!

One word of caution, though. Be sure to get confirmation with someone of a higher frequency so that you know you are on the right path. That person is usually a spiritual healer with a prominent reputation as a spiritual guide, and is someone you can trust to tell you what they see and feel. If you get confirmation after questioning yourself, you know you are on the right track. Cathy and I are two of those people, and are available if you need confirmation, and can be reached at elyce@elycemonet.com.

Many people today call themselves healers, but make sure it is someone you can trust. Don't go to just anyone for them to tell you what you want to hear. A true spiritual guide will tell you the truth in love, even if it hurts.

Some people get caught up in "fighting" the disease, and that isn't the way to go about it. When we are in a "battle" we are creating a separation within ourselves. The way out of the illness is to accept what is. Let's say you have cancer, for example. Accept the cancer as your friend, there to show you what it is you are doing that has caused you to become ill. Healing crises are always there for your good, not to destroy you. It is our lack of acceptance, denial, and fighting it that prevents us from healing! Your genetics are wired to heal. Simply find the root cause of the trauma or teaching that is the original cause, work on healing that, and your healing will happen on its own.

WHAT IS DIVINE HEALING?

In order to begin to heal, we need to become aware that something within us (our mind, our emotions, our human will and/or our body) is out of synch with our divinity (divine blueprint) and needs to be recalibrated. Many times, we turn to Creator when we get sick or someone we love is struggling with health issues. This is a natural and commendable thing to do. It shows that we know deeply somehow that we are connected to Creator and need healing for ourselves and others that is beyond our ability. But the truth is, the ability lies within us. Every cell within us has Creator within it. We are co-creators with God. We don't need to look outward for God... we need to look inward for God. It doesn't mean that you are everything God is. It means that you have everything you need within you, and can create health and well-being through positive intentions, thoughts, feelings and actions.

So, let's start at the beginning. As human beings, we are born in a binary system. It's a state of duality – with both human and divine natures. But it wasn't always that way. We were once in a physically, emotionally and spiritually perfect divine state, made in Creator's image. Something happened that caused that state to "fall" into darkness. Many religious myths talk about sin. Some people believe it was extra terrestrial beings that interfered with our genetics. Regardless of your belief system, suffice it to say that we now live in duality, with both light (God) natures and dark (human) natures.

Our DNA is known to be a 12-strand helix, however we now only operate on 2 strands! The "fall" from 12 strands to 2 strands, however it happened, was what caused our DNA to be turned off to knowing we are divine. We are now learning that we have co-creative abilities, and that includes turning on the expressions of our genes to the light, instead of being left in the dormancy of the human "fallen" state. Bottom line, we are not "victims" of our genetics, as was once thought by the medical field!

We are becoming more of our divine selves through evolution and involution. What that means is that we have evolved as human beings slowly for thousands of years. It is easy to see how man has evolved from Neanderthal man to who we are today. Our genetics have changed! It is a very slow process, but we are on the verge of huge genetic shifts today. According to many physicists (Bruce Lipton, PhD, Gregg Braden, PhD, and many other scientists) we are poised for huge genetic changes that are coming in these final times. We don't know how long it will take, or when the transition will happen, but we do know that we are being given Divine energies that are coming into our bodies in many ways. These energies can be said to come through the galaxy, emanating through the sun, or coming directly into our bodies from Source and Divine Masters.

What this means relative to health is that our genetics will change through children being born in different, "higher" states. They won't think of themselves as "victims" or act like "victims". They will come in pre-wired to be a higher vibration.

It is critical to understand that all disease entered the world because we are now in a Human DNA state rather than a divine DNA state. Source did not cause disease. Mankind did! Until the DNA (our personal divine DNA Profile) is turned back on, or catalyzed into oneness, we can't heal ourselves. We need to bring the "As Above" (Creator/heavens) to the "So Below" (Man/Earth). That is the Divine illumination into the human body, or the Creator-Mind that resides in the heart.

It is also very important to remember that both masculine and feminine sides of our natures need to be examined and healed. For example, look at how our brains function. The left side of the brain (masculine) is all about wisdom, thoughts, action, logic and processes. The right side of the brain (feminine) is all about understanding, intuition, feeling, creativity and bringing energy into physical form (manifestation). Just as the man creates life through the wisdom of the sperm, so does the woman nurture life within herself, in order to bring understanding and compassion into physical form. It is Creator's design of creation that we need each other and have both masculine and feminine within ourselves. That means that the typical archetype of the human masculine overriding the feminine needs to shift. It is the feminine aspect of God that is finally coming into its time of rulership. Surrendering to it will become absolutely necessary for us to go into higher states. Men and women are truly created to be equal, but they haven't been treated that way since the "fall" into humanity, where men decided to blame the feminine.

In the healing process, it will be necessary to explore our thoughts, feelings, actions, past and reactions in order to become more aware of where we are out of synch with our Divine Blueprint. Understanding the body as being more than just physical is necessary in order to heal. As we open our hearts to Divine Healing of mind, emotions, and spirit, we catalyze our genetic keys to higher vibrational light codes that trigger a chemical process in our cells to bring healing so that we can free ourselves of disease and live in a higher state of being.

DNA & ANCESTRAL HEALING

We are all connected to Creator and to each other through our DNA. Until we understand that each of us is connected to everyone and everything Creator created, we will not be able to go beyond our ancestral wounding, and that includes the genetics of diseased states. That's why we are born with predispositions to disease.

I find it very intriguing that for years scientists said that we had two stranded DNA and lots of useless "junk" DNA. That junk DNA carries a lot more than we knew! They have since retracted their statements about our disorganized DNA being "junk". In fact, they now believe it may hold within it the decoding of the evolution of our species. They also retracted their belief that DNA was set in stone. It is now scientifically proven that we can change our DNA. That's good news! That means that any negative genetic patterns that we inherited through DNA from our ancestors can be overcome.

Many believe that this junk DNA is being reorganized into a third strand of DNA through the chemical mutative process of our cells. Think about it. Then, instead of operating on a dualistic or binary system, we would operate as a trinity. And does it make sense that our DNA may once have been a 3-stranded helix before the fall? Or just maybe there were more than 3? Is it something we can reclaim?

Perhaps as a civilization we need to mutate a few more thousand years. However, we are beginning to see this new DNA become part of our reality. There is documentation about at least one child born with 3 strands of DNA. Scientists are also finding that our DNA is mutating as a species, and we are capable of 12 full strands of DNA. Check out the following link for the facts.

http://myscienceacademy.org/2013/01/23/scientists-finally-present-evidence-on-expanding-dna-strands/

The important thing to deal with now is the fact that something in our DNA has been lying dormant. I'm going to call this "human DNA", and I am going to call our turned on spiritually DNA "Creator DNA". No, we don't have separate sets of DNA; we simply forgot our connection to Creator! That has brought us much pain and suffering, all which is based in fear. It takes a remembering, an "awakening" or "enlivening" of our DNA in order to be connected to Creator and heal ourselves. This is not a one-time profession of faith in church. This goes much deeper and is connected to spiritual growth as the precursor to good health in a biological sense.

Once our DNA becomes activated in our "Divine" state, we have within us the power to heal ourselves. Without it, there is only what mankind has created and determined from the human mind to heal the physical reality. The human mind is simply a computer that processes garbage in-garbage out and forms decisions based on experience. The problem is that healing without Creator is like trying to mend a tear in a box by using the same methods that created the tear! Conversely, when we allow the light (Creator) to enliven our DNA, we have the same abilities to heal as Jesus did. Miracles happen!

We must REMEMBER and ACT UPON Divine Truth within us in order to release our fallen state and return to our original Creator-DNA. This is the act of making the decision to accept our shadows and walk in a new way.

Our higher spiritual truths are manifest through a process of each individual's own unique journey of awareness, transformation and transmutation. We are exhorted biblically to be transformed by the renewing of our minds on a minute by minute basis. We are saved by grace, minute by minute! It is NOT a one-time profession of faith that gives us the ability to heal ourselves. That is simply the beginning of the journey

We must take action minute by minute to go into our hearts and make mental decisions from there (the heart-mind). If we simply choose to use religion and make a profession of faith, we will fall flat. The heart is the only thing Creator cares about! And we can't continue in growth until we embody this truth with heart and mind.

Did you know that the heart has its own mind? Look at the Heart Math Center online and see all the research about the power of the heart. Scientific evidence suggests that the heart is FAR MORE POWERFUL than the mind alone.

As we begin to heal, it is not only a biological process, but a spiritual one that is encoded in the very fabric of our existence as humans.

A MEDICAL PERSPECTIVE

Many scientists, holistic practitioners and medical doctors now believe and understand that trauma is what creates all illness and dis-ease in the body, and it can happen at many levels; physical, emotional, psychological, environmental, spiritual, and semantic (which includes ancestral). These traumas are also cumulative; they remain in the body until they are cleared. Thousands of books have been written on the subject, mainly by those physicians who have gone deeply into healing on a DNA level. We invite you to check out the works of Richard Gerber, M.D., Bruce Lipton, Ph.D. (Biology of Belief), Richard Rudd (Gene Keys), Gregg Braden (Spontaneous Healing of Belief), Christian Fleche, (Biodecoding), Patrick Obissier, Keith Scott- Mumby, MD., Ph.D., etc. just to name a few.

Traumas happen every day, beginning in the womb and continuing throughout our lives. Trauma can be a biological organism (flu, cold, illness, etc.) a physical injury, an environmental incident (toxic air, radiation, electromagnetic interference, etc.), emotional pain that wounded us, and more. When the body has traumas, it can't correct it will automatically compensate and adapt. Over time, this compromises our immune system, and our body gets sick from the toxic overload.

Getting well does not necessarily mean you have cleared the trauma; it simply means your body stores it in an organ somewhere so you can continue to function. Once the body can no longer compensate and adapt you will become symptomatic and an illness will express itself. Our goal is to go to the root issue of the illness and cleanse it completely on a cellular level so that the illness doesn't return.

We are all electrical beings. It is now agreed upon in the traditional medical field that our bio field (auric field) is electric. So much for the "woo woo" aura readers! They had it right all the time! I guess they had to be the ones to bring it forth and be laughed at for decades before the traditional societies could accept it as truth. Now the auric field or electrical bio field, as it is called in medical circles, is part of the medical system. You might be interested to know that most everything in the body is electric! Even the chemical processes in the body take electricity to create the chemical reaction. The medical community at large has been treating the biochemical aspects of the body and has largely ignored the electrical until recently, with some exceptions.

Because traumas are electrical frequencies, they operate on frequency levels, and can alter our DNA. Think in terms of polarities and magnets. One magnet attracts in another magnet and they stick together and become one. The truth is that is exactly what we do. We have a trauma, and it acts like a magnet and connects with the frequency we carry in our DNA code. I personally struggled with this until I understood it may or may not be something I am DOING. It may just be happening because it is in my ancestral DNA. You see, we also carry out ancestors' traumas through our DNA. This is what is meant in the bible by "the iniquities of the fathers are visited upon the children". It is through our DNA!

Another thing scientists have learned about DNA is that it is constantly interacting with our mind, will and emotions, as well as our external or environmental conditions, as written in articles by Grazyna Fosar and Franz Bluudorf. Here are excerpts:

"THE HUMAN DNA IS A BIOLOGICAL INTERNET *and superior in many aspects to the artificial one. There is evidence for a whole new type of medicine in which*

DNA can be influenced and reprogrammed by words and frequencies WITHOUT cutting out and replacing single genes.

Only 10% of our DNA is being used for building proteins. It is this subset of DNA that is of interest to western researchers and is being examined and categorized. The other 90% are considered "junk DNA." The Russian researchers, however, convinced that nature was not dumb, joined linguists and geneticists in a venture to explore those 90% of "junk DNA."

Their results, findings and conclusions are simply revolutionary! According to them, our DNA is not only responsible for the construction of our body but also serves as data storage and in communication. The Russian linguists found that the genetic code, especially in the apparently useless 90%, follows the same rules as all our human languages. To this end they compared the rules of syntax (the way in which words are put together to form phrases and sentences), semantics (the study of meaning in language forms) and the basic rules of grammar. The Russian biophysicist and molecular biologist Pjotr Garjajev and his colleagues also explored the vibrational behavior of the DNA. The bottom line was: "Living chromosomes function just like solitonic/ holographic computers using the endogenous DNA laser radiation."

"This means that they managed for example to modulate certain frequency patterns onto a laser ray and with it influenced the DNA frequency and thus the genetic information itself. One can simply use words and sentences of the human language! This, too, was experimentally proven! Living DNA substance (in living tissue, not in vitro) will always react to language-modulated laser rays and even to radio waves, if the proper frequencies are being used."

What science found in deep human biological study was something Christ and the Essenes already knew and practiced! We can change our DNA and our bodies at all levels through prayer, meditation, confession, plants (healing oils) and by changing our thoughts and emotional patterns by reaching for Creator. I call it Sacred or Divine Healing. Funny that it has taken us more than 2000 years to discover something that was accepted and practiced so long ago. It just goes to prove that when we are operating in our human blueprint, we are a little slow!

ESSENTIAL TRUTHS FOR HEALING YOURSELF

Have you ever noticed that when you put your mind and heart to something, you can usually accomplish it? That's because **WHERE YOU FOCUS YOUR MIND AND HEART IS WHAT YOU CREATE/ MANIFEST.**

So, what is focus? You will hear the word "consciousness" a lot. I used to be a little confused by that word, not understanding what it meant, until I learned that it is the same thing as where I put the attention of my mind and heart - FOCUS. Our FOCUS is our conscious mind using its Creator-given power to create. Everything in your world is and has been created by you, either with or without Creator, by design or by default. It is high time we begin to understand the truth of the power within us. We are creating our reality whether we know it or not, with every thought, with every emotion, and with every action. If you want to see what your belief system is, look around you at your creation! The way you live, the way you spend your money, the people in your life and your relationship to them, your work, your choices, all reflect your belief system and where you have FOCUSED or NOT FOCUSED your energy. That's right... when you are in an UN-FOCUSED state, you are still creating... from your *subconscious*. Your outer world is a reflection of all the choices you made from your inner belief system, and many times you are creating without consciously being aware of it. When the subconscious mind is in control without the FOCUSED

GUIDANCE of the conscious mind, we repeat old habits, patterns and traumas. Funny thing is that we can't figure out why we keep getting the same negative result! It's because we are allowing our subconscious habits and patterns to create our reality. Conscious co-creation of the life we want starts with taking responsibility for ourselves and understanding and believing in the power we truly have. It is Creator's Gift!

Many people deny responsibility for illness and negative circumstances, blaming others… even Creator! It's time to change. We can't heal if we don't take responsibility! Creator didn't make you sick… you made you sick from years of bad habits and patterns. Most times, Creator didn't afflict you. In fact, even in the book of Job, it states that Creator allowed Satan to buffet Job. Creator didn't afflict him. Satan did. But Creator allowed it. Sometimes that is what it takes to become aware of our values and choices in life. Many times, you have made choices based on what you were conditioned to believe, and you were not acting out of your higher self or Divine blueprint. It's o.k. We all do it. Once you take responsibility for having created your situation or illness, you can confess it, cleanse it, and bring compassion to yourself. Forgiving yourself for what you didn't know is all part of the process. We aren't meant to focus on our mistakes, (when we focus there we create more mistakes!) but rather on the **truth of who we really are and where we want to be.**

Yeshua (Jesus) gave us the keys to consciously co-create our life WITH CREATOR, rather than allowing our subconscious habits and patterns to carry us along in the drift of life. He was our perfect example of how to do it, by focusing his mind on the things of Creator rather than the things of this world. When we do that, we can co-create a divine existence that heals every aspect of our lives. But it takes work! We must be consciously aware of what we are doing and change it!

Creator is light and in Him there is no darkness at all. If we become aware of our mistakes and seek to change them, we are immediately cleansed. Cleansing and purification of our negative thoughts, habits, patterns and projections are key to healing! Once we forgive ourselves for our mistakes, we can forgive others.

The prescription for eliminating illness is simple:

1) Become **AWARE** of our need for Creator by examining our thoughts, emotions and environments in which we find ourselves. (Hearing the Still, Small Voice within. This can also be called intuition.)
2) **AWAKEN** to the truth of what needs to be changed in our lives. (Take responsibility for what we have done.)
3) Take **ACTION to** purify ourselves, which is the act of confessing and forsaking whatever is out of alignment and making amends with people we have hurt or traumatized.

Once we activate our divine blueprint within (awaken to our Creator-DNA by confessing and releasing our "shadow" pattern of victim consciousness that feels separate from Creator) then we are cleansed by light and the healing begins.

Our perfect example is Jesus, of course, who gave us many examples of healing. He healed lepers, those paralyzed, a woman hemorrhaging, the blind, the lame, those oppressed by demons, and even raising people from the dead. They are recorded in the Gospels and are easy to find. But he also taught the disciples, who also began healing themselves and others. You can do the same thing today. Heal yourself by tapping into your co-creational abilities within you!

UNDERSTANDING THE STEPS

So now that you are ready to heal, I want to share 3 stages in the healing process already revealed in the last chapter.

PHASE 1: AWARENESS (The voice of who we are being)

PHASE 2: AWAKENING (The belief and responsibility of who we are being)

PHASE 3: ACTION (Creating conscious actions based on truth to affect a positive outcome)

So, let's define what each of these phases is about.

Phase 1: AWARENESS

The first phase of healing requires understanding that I have both a conscious and subconscious mind. The conscious mind is like the captain of the ship giving orders, and the subconscious mind is the engine crew that actually does the work from below deck that no one sees. The crew (your subconscious mind) is always there and is always working. It is aware of memories, emotions and traumas that are available to recall. It is also in constant contact with your unconscious mind, which is the part of our consciousness we can't recall by ourselves. For the purpose of healing with Genetic Oil Elixirs™ let's discuss and work with the conscious and subconscious minds.

The best way to become aware is to enter into a state of prayer and meditation and ask your higher self for the truth to probing questions about why we are experiencing this and that. Then we need to listen for our heart's answer. That is NOT the negative voice inside your head telling you nasty things about yourself. That is from the dark, ignorant side! Ignore it. The answers I am talking about come from your heart, and tell you that you are loved and nothing can separate you from love. It offers gentle and loving guidance into the truth of our shadow side or human mistakes.

Phase 2: AWAKENING

The second phase of healing involves accepting the truth about who we are BEING. It is important to note that we are called human beings, not human doings. We have been so conditioned by the world to think that who we are is based on what we do. However, the truth is that our lives are created by our thoughts and emotions, followed by our actions. If we want to change and heal ourselves, we start with who we are BEING. What we think, how we feel, what charges us into action both positively and negatively. The still, small voice within us has given us information about ourselves. Now we have to ask, "Is it truth?" This is the phase that takes much courage, and becomes the activator of our Creator DNA. If we are willing to face ourselves, and surrender our human will to our divine will, then the awakening and grace will pour into us and enliven every cell within our bodies with light. We will be given divine power to change anything we need to change within ourselves.

We must have the courage to admit to ourselves the truth and come out of denial. If we don't, there will be no healing. If we do, we are unstoppable, capable of changing our lives in every way we desire!

Some people have been so closed off from their inner voice that they have trouble hearing the truth in their heart. There are several ways to address this: 1) Continue on in prayer, asking for grace to hear the truth 2) Get a Spiritual Coach who can assist you in understanding what Spirit is saying and assist you to move at a pace that is comfortable for you. Having a guide is sometimes very helpful, since we are all somewhat blinded to our own shadow side. It helps to have an objective, trained coach or pastor who can give you assistance. I have done this work for years and work with other Spiritual Healers whom you can interview. Simply email elyce@ elycemonet.com for information.

Phase 3: ACTION

The third phase is ONGOING ACTION. Once you are committed to awakening, you must take steps forward! This involves prayer and meditation, awareness of your mistakes, and making amends when necessary. It sounds so simple, yet we make it so complicated! The action steps must be repeated and embodied if we are to change our lives. Step by step instructions follow in the next chapter.

Action also involves visualization, a technique that has been used for thousands of years to "see" Creator at work. It is not done with your physical eyes, but rather with your eyes closed and through the imagination. Visualization helps us to see ourselves as healed, and to feel the effects of that healing in our bodies. It also sets up the mind to positively accept the healing and believe it to be truth. If the mind does not believe it, the healing will not take place. It is important to visualize ourselves as we want to be in order to co-create our new, healthy state.

DOING IT!

STEPS TO PHASE 1 – AWARENESS

Find A Quiet Place. Sit in a comfortable chair with your feet firmly planted on the floor and your palms up in your lap. (Attitude of surrender) A quiet, undistracted environment is necessary to go deep within.

Apply Genetic Healing Oils Elixirs™ and visualize yourself as perfectly healthy! Bring focus to the area that is ill or traumatized. Pray.

Look at the Oil Descriptions to discover which oils feel right for your purpose. Trust your intuition! Use the manual to see where to apply the oils.

Next, ask for the truth from your heart on the answers to these questions:

> **Where has my focus been on this issue? (ON MYSELF, ON OTHERS)**

> Am I being selfish or do I lack boundaries for myself? Am I operating consciously or subconsciously?

> **Who am I being? (VICTIM, JUDGE, RESCUER)**

It is important to understand that we all play all three, although we have a default to one of them most of the time. When we are able to see ourselves in each role, we can clear the negative habits and patterns. Here are some descriptions of each role:

Victim – I see others (and/or Creator) as hurting me. I am in self-pity. Negative emotion attached is usually sadness, depression, anxiety, anger.

Judge – I see others (and/or Creator) as hurting me and make them bad and wrong for what they are doing. Negative emotion attached is usually frustration, anger, rage, indignance or intolerance.

Rescuer – Others (and/or Creator) can't do things without me. Negative emotion attached is usually seen as interference, control, over nurturing and overly sympathetic.

What is my belief system around this issue? (Is there an old belief system that is ready to be acknowledged and changed?)

Remember when I said your STATE OF BEING has everything to do with your healing? By becoming aware of where my focus is and who I am being, I can begin to discover the hidden belief system that is buried in my subconscious and is causing me misalignment with my Divine Blueprint.

STEPS IN PHASE 2: AWAKENING

Listen to the messages that come through (in meditation and from people you trust) about who you are being.

Feel it DEEPLY and own it.

> **Feel the pain of being separate from Creator in this place. Ask yourself, "Am I ready to surrender to change?"**

> Awakening to Creator is about finding the truth about ourselves. As we face our own demons and traumas head on, we find that they aren't as scary as we think they are!

> If we aren't willing to look and accept them as being real, we can't heal. It is all about owning the truth of our own darkness, and having compassion for ourselves that all humans have this need to face themselves where they deny Creator. Most times, we have only done it out of fear.

> Focus on your desire to change, having compassion for yourself. We all fall short as humans, and there must be a healthy balance between deeply knowing the pain we have created in ourselves and others and forgiving ourselves for it.

Awakening is the part that takes the most courage. Awakening is a soul choice. If you don't accept the awareness deep into your heart as truth you will not be able to effect change. You can even take drastic measures externally, but it won't work with Creator. Creator cannot be manipulated. He knows if your heart is true. If it is not, you will continue to recycle old habits and patterns until you come to the end of yourself! So be mindful of the opportunities we have to awaken. Hold them as precious. You are being called by the Creator of the Universe in this time and place of your life. Listen. Face your demons (literally and metaphorically), and then take action toward change.

It isn't about perfection; it is about the willingness of your soul to surrender to your higher self.

STEPS IN PHASE 3: ACTION

Anoint yourself with Genetic Healing Oil Elixirs™

See Chapters on Application

Pray a Prayer of Awareness of your Shadow

See Chapter on Specific Prayers you can use and adapt, or just pray to Creator from your heart.

Ask Creator what Action you need to take to create this new way of being.

Your initial request may bring forth one or two steps you are to take immediately.

Thereafter, you need to repeat anointing and praying daily in order to walk in newness of life. If we don't ask for daily help, we will simply fall back into old patterns.

Modern psychology has determined that it takes 21 days for a new practice to become a habit (or embodied into our subconscious). We must consider our old habit as rendered powerless, although the mind loop will still be running. We cannot erase a mind loop. We can only create a new one. ***So, for a minimum of 21 days, anointing, prayer, meditation and action are needed to create total change in your life.***

THE POWER OF RELATIONSHIPS

One thing I have come to know intimately is that relationships are where we truly reveal ourselves for who we are being in any given moment. This means that every relationship in your life has the power to transform your illness.

You have heard about The Law of Attraction. This is simply a modern version of a Universal Truth of how we are designed; our inside life is reflected in our outside life so that we can see who we are being. What I have learned is that who we are being (from our subconscious mind) may be exhibited rather than what we want to be exhibited. This is often the case.

We are so programmed and conditioned that we are on auto-pilot. We need to become more and more aware of what we are saying, what we are thinking and what we are doing. It all starts with awareness and the vulnerability that says, "I don't know it all. I can open my mind to hear your heart and what you are saying behind your words. I am willing to be wrong. I am willing to learn something new about myself and about you."

Our lifetime is all about learning who we truly are. Creator has designed us so that we attract in the same frequency at which we are vibrating, or we attract in the frequency that is the opposite of what we are vibrating so that we can mirror back to ourselves our own pattern.

In my life, the most important mirrors were my relationships, and I have come to learn that this is truth for all. It begins with our relationship to Creator and extends to our primary intimate relationships (husband/wife), then to our children, our coworkers and friends, and so on.

The victim pattern for me was a significant one. I kept attracting more and more abusers until I figured out that I was playing the victim! Once I owned the victim-ness of my own thoughts, I was able to go beyond playing the role and the abuse stopped. I realized that I was not creating proper boundaries for myself. When I created boundaries and held them, the abusers stopped abusing and I attracted in a higher quality relationship.

Most people will find themselves in one of the roles most comfortably. Since the victim state is the state of non-self – responsibility, it is the one most of us are utilizing.

How we treat those we are closest to is usually the most telling of where we need to do healing work on ourselves. Don't worry. Everyone is this way and you are not unique. It is simply Creator's design to help us to see ourselves in the mirrors of those closest to us so that we can begin to accept where we are out of alignment. What it means, though, is that it is time to put down your pride and defensiveness. Creator already sees your pride and arrogance. It is no secret! It is you who is hiding--- from yourself.

Relationships are the most important part of life. When you think about it, everything is about relationship. How I relate to my partner. How I relate to my kids. How I relate to my siblings. How I relate to my customers in business. How I relate to government. How I relate to my dog. How I relate to nature. How I relate to people who disagree with me. How I relate to those of different color and belief systems. Everything in life is a virtual learning ground when it comes to relationships. It is the most complex place for awakening, and so Creator uses it to help us find truth and light.

I exhort you to look at your relationships first. Where are you being dogmatic? Where are you insisting that you are right and others wrong?

What are other people saying to you? In my own awakening process, one of my children told me that I was the one of the most judgmental people she had ever known. That hurt my heart so badly, I went straight to Creator! And I learned she was right! Many years ago, I had adopted a pattern of right and wrong, good and bad, and had forgotten compassion. I had projected my own control onto others and blamed them. I had become a judge or persecutor to avoid playing the victim. This was a very important step for my healing.

You can believe that I owned it and asked for forgiveness and strength to be more accepting of others and to be able to own my own negative traits. Learning to love ourselves involves the acceptance of our dark side. And in my case, I was raised with the belief system that we control our external circumstances to get what we want and to prove we are right. The problem was that it didn't work in relationships. I was forced to look inward and let go of my genetic patterning and face myself. It wasn't easy, but it was worth it. My relationships with my children transformed, as did all my relationships.

It is all part of the fodder for growth. We all have blind spots. We can see others much more clearly than we can see ourselves.

Where are you hiding? What are other people close to you saying about you? Are you listening? Are you willing to see one iota of truth in what they are saying? If you are, you can transcend the darkness within yourself and your life will take on new meaning. You will have peace, respect, and love surrounding you. I am living proof!

A Note About Change

Resistance from others is always to be expected. Very often those closest to you will scoff and mock you in your attempts to be honest. Don't despair. Stay at it, realizing that no one likes change! But as we continue to work on ourselves, we will heal emotionally, mentally, spiritually and physically and our relationships will begin to reflect that change. Stick with it! Perseverance will be needed to heal. Keep telling yourself you are worth it! In time, your loved ones will see that it is real and start honoring your efforts.

CASE STUDIES AS EXAMPLES

(All cases are fictional and are for the purpose of example only)

CASE STUDY #1 – MEET MARY

Mary is a homemaker raising 3 children. She loves her husband and children and does everything for them. Mary works day and night to take care of raising the kids. She keeps a clean house. She goes to church on Sunday and makes sure to volunteer in church activities monthly. She washes and starches her husband's dress shirts because he likes it the way Mom used to do it. She creates all organic meals for the family, because she wants them to be healthy, but she snacks all day on chips and fast food, because she is so busy driving kids to school and cleaning house and doing laundry and running errands, that she can't find the time for herself to eat healthy. When her husband comes home, she has his dinner prepared, but she resents that he doesn't see how much she works on his behalf. She hears her mother's voice, "It's always better to give than to receive". She tries so hard to be kind to her husband and to her kids, but every now and then Mary breaks down and runs to her room feeling unappreciated and unloved, and ends up with a migraine. She works tirelessly and seems to get nothing in return. She gives and gives and gives, but she finds herself 30lbs overweight, wearing the same clothes every week (the kids and husband need new clothes more than she does, and besides she wants to lose weight before she buys new) and her hair is beginning to go gray. She can tell her husband doesn't find her attractive anymore, and their sex life is almost non-existent. Because of her neediness, she pours herself into her children to find love. Mary decides she can't take the migraines anymore and needs to find answers from Creator.

Here are some answers Mary might receive based on doing the AAA program with an open heart that wants answers through prayer.

Phase I: AWARENESS FOR MARY

Where has my focus been?

Mary, your focus has been on others and not yourself. You are not being selfish, but you lack boundaries. It would do you good to find some boundaries so that you are not giving yourself up completely and then resenting it.

Who am I being? (Victim, Judge, Rescuer)

True, you are being a servant, but is it out of true love or codependence? When you aren't honest about your true feelings, and you are serving others and not taking care of yourself, you are being a people pleaser.

Mary examines her inner negative dialogue to separate feelings from fact and to find the truth:

Mary's Victim: Mary's inner dialogue goes like this: "My husband and children don't see how much I do for them. No one shows me love and I show them love all the time. I give and give and give and get nothing in return."

> a. **Is it truth?** Yes and no. Mary has the power to change all this by being honest with those she loves and taking back her power instead of giving it away. She has trained them that she is only supposed to give and not receive. The responsibility is hers.

Mary's Judge: Mary's inner dialogue goes like this: "They don't deserve all my love. They are selfish and I am not. I am so angry inside, and they are giving me a migraine."

> b. **Is it truth?** No. She loves her family, which is why she wants to serve them. She doesn't love herself! The migraines are from her struggle within herself to be loved, and from deep seated, unexpressed anger and resentment.

Mary's Rescuer: Mary's inner dialogue goes like this: "My family would fall apart if I wasn't here to take care of everything. They are too busy to accomplish these things without me. I am supposed to serve their every need if I am a good wife and mother."

> c. **Is it truth?** No. All families can adjust to new routines, new behaviors with each other, and new levels of respect when they are discussed. No one is indispensable. Divorces and family battles happen

all the time, even when people think they are doing the right thing.

What is my belief system around this issue? (Is there an old belief system that is ready to be acknowledged and changed?)

As soon as Mary asked for angelic assistance, she heard her mother's voice in her head telling her "Mary, it is more blessed to give than to receive." She remembered how pressured she felt to always be the perfect, giving little girl. Mary realizes that her mother taught Mary how to martyr herself, teaching her the extreme of the truth that it is more blessed to give than to receive. Mary realized her Mom did the same thing in the family, and had set a pattern for Mary. She began martyring herself, acting out of this distorted truth, rather than from unconditional love.

Mary has now heard the truth. She has become aware of the roles she has been playing and what is behind it.

Where are you unaware? Are you ready to open your heart to receive the truth before Creator? If so, you will begin to understand that you are no longer a victim of your illness, your circumstances, and others. Go for it! Be vulnerable! Creator already knows who you are and what you need. Call on Creator the Father, Mother and Son to hear your prayer and open your heart to truth. THEN FACE IT! Mary did it, and so can YOU. Mary's next step is PHASE 2: AWAKENING.

PHASE 2: AWAKENING FOR MARY

Mary has just been given the truth from Creator within her. She now must ask herself the big question, **"Am I ready to surrender to change?"**

It is now her decision to feel it deeply within (even the negative emotion of it) and take full responsibility for her actions. She must go beyond her pride and surrender herself naked before Creator. Emotions play a huge part here, as we must go into the negative feelings of what who we have been being to get to the truth of our misalignment. It isn't comfortable, but it is necessary for healing. This is where Mary can either fall back into her negative pattern of blaming others or muster up enough courage to face herself deeply and ask Creator to help her change.

AWAKENING is the point of agreement with Creator about what we are really doing. Only when we are in the place of fully accepting our mistakes can we be cleansed of them. This is the point where we can either enliven our DNA and upgrade it or leave it in a disempowered, fallen human state. The process may take a little time, but the longer we sit in the pain, the worse it feels. The answer is going into the pain and facing it. The sooner you go through it, the faster you go into the light and peace. Choose to make a decision to awaken your Divine DNA in that moment and don't give the darkness an opportunity to steal the truth from you by planting negative thoughts in your mind! You are now in the spiritual battleground. Your decision at this point determines your action steps.

> When Mary asked herself if this was truth, she remembered Jesus' words in her mind. ***"I desire mercy, not sacrifice.' For I have not come to call the righteous, but sinners."***

> As bad as it felt, Mary knew it was the truth. She admitted to herself that giving herself up was her own doing. She knew her husband and family loved her, and she wasn't being honest with them about how she felt. She decided she didn't want to play the victim, the judge or the rescuer any longer. She wanted to be honest with herself. She wanted to change her inner life so her outer life could change. She believed

that she could have a life that included love for herself and boundaries. She told herself that it was o.k., and that she was ready to let go of the negative thoughts and belief systems that were no longer working for her. Mary's tears were real, which is often the case when we realize and accept responsibility for the games we have played. Some call it repentance. Mary surrendered to higher truth. Now she must take action.

Where have you been unwilling to face the truth? Awakening means taking full responsibility for everything in our lives. If we truly see others and our surroundings as a mirror image of what we are doing, it makes sense. We can change our outer surroundings by being aware of and awakening to the truth that we create it all! Now you have a choice to move it out of your life. This is where it gets exciting!

Let's see how Mary does it.

PHASE 3: ACTION FOR MARY

In Mary's case, here is what it might have looked like:

Anoint yourself with Genetic Oil Elixirs*

Mary selected Gold, Frankincense and Myrrh, recognizing her initiation and commitment to change. Then she added Oils of Courage in order to be able to speak her truth in love to her family. Then she added Oils of Solomon for wisdom and protection.

Pray a Prayer of your awareness of what you are doing. (Confession)

Mary selected a prayer on Loving Herself and speaking her truth. See Chapter on Specific Prayers you can use and adapt, or just pray to Creator from your heart.

Ask you higher self what Action you need to take to create this new way of being.

Mary asked and was given a number of answers through her intuition.

a) Mary could talk to her husband about her realization that she has become over-caring and over-serving, being careful not to blame him in any way, and asking for his support to find balance for herself.

b) She can begin to create a regimen for herself that includes a 20-minute prayer and meditation time before anyone gets up in the morning. She can anoint herself with Genetic Oil Elixirs®™ to catalyze the light in her DNA. She can then tune in to her higher self and begin loving herself and healing her imbalance of people pleasing daily.

c) Mary must be diligent about her thoughts and emotions. She needs to let all negative thoughts and emotions pass through her without sticking! It's like she can allow them to operate without focusing on them. She can redirect or CONSCIOUSLY FOCUS her thoughts to a higher truth and her emotions will follow. If she waits for her emotions to change, she will be stuck and go back down the black hole of self-pity and hopelessness. Sometimes declarations can help. I AM LOVED. I AM POWERFUL. IT IS LOVE TO HOLD BOUNDARIES FOR

MYSELF. I AM NOT BEING SELFISH BY HOLDING BOUNDARIES.

c) She can begin to take steps toward loving herself. She can watch her diet, and lose weight. She can begin doing something with her hair and clothes that fit within the family budget and make her feel more beautiful.

d) Mary needs to visualize herself being healed, and feeling happy and loved. When she can continue to see herself this way, she will retrain the mind to create it.

The bottom line is Mary needs to work on her own higher self -esteem (the truth of who she is), and learn what it feels like for to love herself unconditionally. Then she will be ready to truly love others in a way that honors HERSELF as well as her family.

As Mary puts this into practice, within 21 days she will begin to see change in her external environment with her family.

What happens when Mary meets resistance?

Resistance from others is always to be expected. No one likes change! But as Mary continues to take care of her own healing, her emotional life will be uplifted. She will feel happier and will create better health for herself. Her husband and family will begin to see the changes in Mary, and will respond accordingly. They only want her happy! It is all within Mary's power, as she finds happiness in balanced service. Mary must be willing to trust Creator for the outcome.

What about you? Are you willing to suffer through the resistance in order to find peace and well-being? It is a necessary step for us all in order to reach our goal of health.

CASE STUDY #2 – MEET JOHN

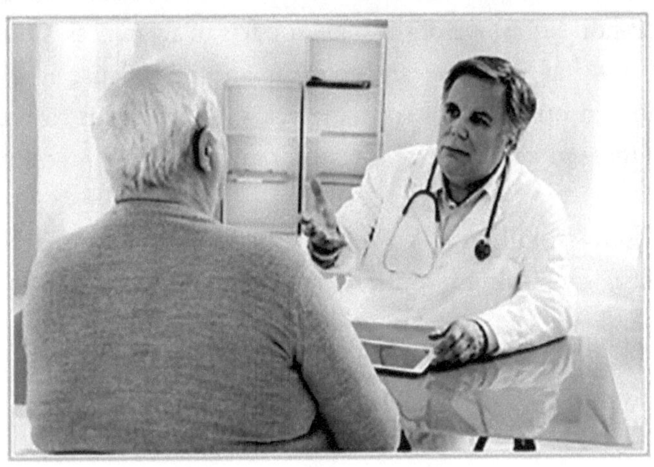

John was just diagnosed with Type 2 Diabetes. His doctor says if he doesn't change his life he will die. He is 50 lbs. overweight, and works as a mechanical engineer at a computer 6 days a week, 10-12 hours a day. By the time he gets home, the rest of the family has eaten, so he stops and grabs a burger and fries and soft drink or other fast food most nights. When he was growing up, he and his Mom ate fast food a lot, as a reward for an achievement. Dad wasn't around because he was always working. That was ok, because Dad gave John nice things. This was the way his parents rewarded him.

John's wife has begged him to stop working so hard, seeing the stress in his face, knowing he has high blood pressure and high cholesterol on top of it all. She has been trying to give him supplements and ways he can bring down his blood pressure and cholesterol and shows him articles on diet and its effects on his conditions, but he turns a deaf ear. She also sees the family falling apart, because their teenagers don't have Dad home most of the time. She is angry with John and is ready to leave him and take the boys.

It is time for John to ask himself some serious questions. John is at a critical place. If he faces this, it could save his life. If he doesn't, he risks losing his wife and kids and ultimately his health even to a point of death. While he has been in distinct denial, if John is willing to go deep and do the work, he can expect miraculous results.

Self-honesty is one of the biggest parts of awareness. Our minds can tell us that what we are doing is alright because it has been acceptable in our lives for so many years. What needs to happen is a willingness to surrender to Creator, pray with a heart to know the truth.

If John is willing to go into his heart and call on Creator, he might hear something like the story I have created in the following pages.

PHASE I: AWARENESS FOR JOHN

Where has John's focus been?

John's focus has been on himself. Sure, he brings home the bacon, but he has never shared himself through his heart and his time. Is he being selfish? Yes. And it has become self-destructive and ended up as a medical illness. Obviously, John has been focused on his job. He is being a mechanical engineer, allowing that to define who he is. Why? He spends time there because he gets something from it. He receives accolades for being a good engineer on his job. His ego gets stroked. He also makes good money. It is really more about the ego though, because he has plenty of money now after all these years, and doesn't have to work the hours he works.

John, your focus has been entirely on yourself. You are being selfish and not listening or being concerned about others.

Who is John being? (Victim, Judge, Rescuer)

John is being a left-brained, logical man who has not opened himself up to Creator, which causes his DNA to be dormant. Even though he calls himself a Christian, attending church weekly. His heart and emotions have not been a part of his life. He is focused entirely on serving his own desires and ego. John has made his work his life, instead of having a balanced existence that includes his wife and family. The only joy he gets is from his job. He has forgotten how to relate to people and has buried himself in his computer. It's easier when he doesn't have to communicate, and he does as he pleases to indulge his food cravings.

John's Victim: John's inner dialogue goes like this: "My wife and kids don't understand how hard I work to put food on the table. They don't appreciate me at all. I pay all the bills, they live in a gorgeous home and have luxury cars, and they don't understand that all that is because of me.

   a. **Is it truth?** No. John is closing himself off to the family and doing what strokes his ego. He must open to considering what others feel and what his part of the problem is, rather than blaming others.

We are all connected, and designed to be in harmony with our relationships and environment. They are our greatest gifts! If you want to heal, you must begin listening to others and seeing that their messages are reflections of who you are being. Use them as MIRRORS.

John's Judge: John's inner dialogue goes like this: "They don't deserve all that I give them. If she wants to leave, she can leave. Then those selfish teenage brats can find out how hard it is to earn a living on their own. I work so hard, I deserve to eat what I want and I don't need anyone telling me differently. Besides, I don't think it will make a difference. Doctors are idiots. I'm not going to die."

> a) Is it truth? Yes and No. John is in delusion. He thinks they can't go on without him and is gambling that the money he provides will keep them from leaving. Eventually, though, his wife and kids won't be able to continue the way things are and they will leave. John needs to be honest with himself. If he continues to be a tyrant and do what is bad for his body, he will end up without a family and it will eventually cost him his life.

John's Rescuer: John's inner dialogue goes like this: "It's time for me to take care of me, and it's ok that I don't want to change. My family would fall apart if I wasn't here to take care of everything. I need to take care of myself in a way that makes me happy. I deserve it."

> a. Is it truth? No. John has every right to make a decision to hurt himself. But really, what victory is there in self-abuse and self-sabotage? What he is saying is he can die if he wants to. This is true. But why would he want to? This type of thinking is not rational.

What is John's belief system? Is there a hidden belief system that is underlying John's behavior?

John has several distorted belief systems. First, he believes it is ok to spend 90% of his time away from his family and not interact with them. He believes his job as a husband and father stops at providing money. Second, he believes it is ok to reward himself with fast food because he works hard, even though it is killing him. Third, he doesn't believe what the doctors are telling him. He is smarter about his health than they are. John is unwilling to learn new things about himself and his health.

Even though John has almost killed himself because of his denial, he is still being given an opportunity to be cleansed through surrender to truth. There is no timeline for healing on Creator's side. It's just that on our side, the longer we wait, the more the damage we do to our physical bodies and the harder it is to reverse. Remember, Creator's other universal truth says we reap what we sow!

If and when John is ready to face himself with an open heart, John might hear something like this:

"John, you are playing God. You are in complete denial and are hurting yourself and others because of your unwillingness to listen. You have not surrendered to Me".

John examines his inner negative dialogue to separate feelings from fact and to find the truth.

a. **What is my belief system around this issue? (Is there an old belief system that is ready to be acknowledged and changed?)**

As soon as John asked for angelic assistance, he got a picture in his mind of him and his mother at a fast food restaurant where he was being honored with food for getting good grades in school. He realized that his Mom had done this to reward him, but he had somehow connected his goodness and appreciation from people with eating fast food. It was a big revelation for John! He wondered if he would be or could be healthier if he changed how he felt about rewarding himself with food. He realized that would help. His wife was trying to show him but didn't know how. He realized he was the one who needed to change.

John then asked if there were other mind patterns that needed changing. He closed his eyes and listened, after anointing himself with Oils of Courage. He got another picture in his mind of being alone as a child, wondering why his Dad didn't love him enough to spend time with him. He instantly was able to see how he had created that same pattern with his kids his father had with him. He had made his work the place that gave him rewards, but he had ignored his children.

John felt horrible. He felt he had failed his family. So now he has the big step of self-forgiveness and taking action to change.

With this manual in hand, John went to the next step... AWAKENING.

PHASE 2: AWAKENING FOR JOHN

John asked himself the big question, **"Am I ready to surrender to change?"**

There is a lot to be surrendered here. His angels and guides are opening him to truth he hasn't been willing to face in 40 years. As he asked for help, John realized how much he had strayed from his spiritual path. He asked the angels and masters to assist him to live in truth, and to be humble and begin to hear the voice of truth. John sobbed deeply. His angels and guides heard the call and came to his side with other angels who assisted in John's healing. They gave John assistance energetically, and John stopped sobbing and asked for forgiveness. He was forgiven in an instant.

After what seemed endless agony, John became a new man. He was in his heart. He had connected to the divinity within himself, and something inside him had changed. He knew now the action he must take.

PHASE 3: ACTION

John anointed himself with Genetic Oil Elixirs™ on his 3rd eye, palms, bottoms of his feet and on his heart. He was clear that he needed to clear his energy centers from his crown to his feet. He selected the following:

Holy Oils of Anointing (3rd Eye) Oil of Solomon (Palms)

Oils of Courage (Heart)

Oil of Magdalene (Feet) Three Kings (neck)

John Prayed. He confessed his denial of Creator. He confessed his need for Creator. Then he prayed according to his written list so he didn't get lost. As he is praying, he is visualizing the energy coming into his body from the top of his head to the bottom of his feet. He is using his imagination to see rays of light that are coming in to heal him, and noting their colors, texture, taste and feel. John prays for the following healing from Creator:

b. Healing of my mind to see the truth
c. Healing of my heart to love myself, my wife and my kids

d. Healing of my physical body
e. Healing of my speech so I can show love
f. Healing of my habits with food
g. Healing of my emotions that need constant reassurance

John Asked Creator what action steps to take, and was given a number of answers:

a. John could ask for a spiritual coach that he can meet with once a week to hold him accountable for change in a positive way.
b. John could go to his wife and share his revelations about himself and ask her forgiveness for his stubbornness and resistance to her love.
c. John could ask forgiveness of his children for not being there.
d. John could set an intention to change his work habits so that he is home at reasonable hours, in time for dinner together with his family.
e. John could set up a meditation daily, so that he can stay out of denial and in his higher self.
f. He could begin to change his diet and eating habits, asking Creator for clearing of the damage he has done to his body.
g. He could make an appointment with the doctor to put him on a plan that will be conducive to healing his diabetes.
h. John could set up a new reward system for himself that includes doing something fun without junk food! He can share it with his wife so they can agree on the rewards (i.e., going to the movies or play golf, or whatever)

What Happens if John Fails?

We all fail in our attempts to change, but we only fail in the minute we fail! Each minute, hour, day offers new opportunity. We are powerless to change unless we are in connection with our divine selves. John needs to remember to surrender his thoughts and feelings daily, and take one day at a time. He could make a journal of his progress so he has a marker that he is really doing it. When he fails, he can have a system for starting over the next day correctly!

NEGATIVE ENTITIES
AND DARK SPIRITS

There is much discussion about how these negative entities and dark spirits came into being. I shall cover two schools of thought.

The first is the evolutionary view. Mankind, in its "fallen" state, creates negative energy through negative thinking and emotions. They become so powerful that they take on a life of their own. Think of television shows like "Lost" that depicted black air that enshrouded beings and killed them off. The black air was the negative energy created by the collective consciousness of fear and projected onto others. This negative energy can become very powerful and can take on many shapes and forms in the human mind. Because God is within us, our awareness of what we are doing, and turning away from it, prevents us from going to the state of the darkness of the collective consciousness. It is precisely the Awareness, Action and Awakening that turns on the DNA and dissipates darkness. In truth, we all have the darkness within us, and we have the capability of calling it in or through our AAA process, diminishing it.

The second is the Biblical view. Jesus addresses very adamantly that there are demons and entities that work against us. He cleared them from people, addressed them by name, and healed people from their possession by them. It must be understood that these entities are real, and are operating at all times. Christian Churches call it "the devil" but in my experience with healing, there are basically 3 categories:

1) Human Ego – Stubbornness that refuses to do what it known to be right. When we continue to act in this way and feed our negative feelings and attitudes, we become prey for the dark. They flock to us to use us, mock us, etc. We become puppets.

2) Negative Entities – Human beings who have died and have not gone to the light. They need light in order to stay in spirit form, so they attach to living beings to suck their energy. Some of them don't mean harm. Sometimes they are simply loved ones who are confused and don't want to leave. Sometimes they are purposely attached to suck from you.

3) Dark Spirits – Demons and Fallen Angels. These are beings that have never incarnated as humans. They are angels who followed Lucifer. The Demons are their henchmen, created by Lucifer with no connection to their hearts or Creator. They only serve the darkness. This was the primary reason for Lucifer's expulsion from Heaven. He was playing Creator.

There is a difference between negative habits and patterns and negative entities and dark spirits. However, when we consistently repeat mistakes and don't turn to Creator for forgiveness, we create a portal of entry for all negative beings. They can go within our spinal columns, organs, central nervous systems, brains, and blood. They can be all pervasive.

All people are subject to attachment and oppression by these entities and spirits. Don't worry! You can be attached and oppressed and not possessed by them. There is a difference. Do know, however, that you are better off getting them cleared because they are detrimental to your thinking and creating joy. They delight in robbing our joy and work hard to create destructive tendencies within us that leave us feeling separate from Creator.

If you are concerned about this, feel free to contact me at elyce@elycemonet.com. I have a network of healers who specialize in this type of work. They are fierce warriors of light who work with guides and angels from beyond the veil to clear these disturbances. They can name the type and organ or structure of attachment. They can also provide protection from future invasion.

Don't think you are above it! We all have had entities and dark spirits. Many times, physical illness is one of the results of infiltration and attachment.

You are not bad and wrong. You are love and light. That is truth. We all carry ancestral fear within our DNA, along with all the negative thought and emotional patterns that go with the histories of our lineage. By investigating and healing it, it may save your life!

A word of warning. Don't seek to clear entities on your own. They won't go by command of their host. It takes spiritual forces of light that are beyond this realm to clear them. A knowledgeable spiritual healer can assist you in this type of clearing. Cathy and I both have this ability and are available to you if needed at elyce@elycemonet.com. Work first on changing your habits and patterns. If you still sense you are being oppressed, contact me and I can arrange a healing.

GENETIC OIL ELIXIRS™

1. **GOLD FRANKINCENSE & MYRRH** were the gifts (frequencies) of the Magi given to Jesus for his initiation into mastery. Gold brings wealth, happiness and comfort. Frankincense & Myrrh were used for purification and healing. They were more expensive than gold. We infuse these oils with *Gold and quartz crystal*, known for purification and magnification.

2. **THREE KINGS** has the essences of Sandalwood, Myrrh, Juniper, Frankincense, and Spruce with Almond Oil. This blend opens the subconscious mind through pineal stimulation. It releases deep seated trauma. It is grounding and spiritually uplifting at the same time. Infused with *Ametrine Elixir*, it brings inner peace and tranquility; it is a vehicle for increased psychic awareness and spiritual enlightenment.

3. **OILS OF COURAGE** contains the essences of Rosewood, Blue Tansy, Frankincense and Almond Oil. This blend was used by Roman soldiers before battle. It has the emotional impact of stimulating courage. Adds confidence, purpose, serenity, communication and self-awareness. We have infused our oils with *Aquamarine Elixir* for added strength and courage.

Genetic Oil Elixirs™

4. **OILS OF GLADNESS** This blend contains Frankincense, Myrrh, Clary Sage, Ylang Ylang, Litsea with Almond Oil. These essences impact the emotional centers of the brain and affect a positive and uplifting feeling. Increases psychic ability and the capacity for inspiration, learning skills and discipline. We have infused the oils with ***Celestite Elixir*** for even higher lifting.

5. **ROSE OF SHARON** This is Cistus the Desert Rock Rose. It heals the wounded heart and opens one up to new emotional experiences. It was used by the ancients to heal wounds, regenerate cells and boost the immune system. We have infused these oils with ***Ruby Elixir*** to send love to the heart.

6. **OIL OF SOLOMON** Frankincense, Myrrh, Galbanum, Cistus and Damascus Rose with Almond Oil imparts wisdom and leadership to the wearer. Solomon used it to connect to the spirit world. It connects the root and crown chakras clearing and aligning all chakras and assists the rise of Kundalini energy (Ascension/Rapture). Infused with ***18 Carat Gold Elixir.***

7. **HOLY ANOINTING OIL** of Moses Exodus 30:23-24. Creator gives Moses and all generations to follow a recipe for anointing oil. It includes: Myrrh, Cassia, Cinnamon, Calamus and First Press Olive Oil. This is the oil given to Aaron and his caste of apothecaries to purify the Temple and the congregation. Jesus sent this oil with his disciples to heal the sick. Infused with ***Rose Quartz Elixir.***

8. **OIL OF THE MAGDALENE** blends Spikenard, Myrrh, and organic almond oil. This is the blend used by Mary Magdalene on the feet of Jesus before the crucifixion. It alleviates pain, fear, and anxiety. It can be used for deep meditation. Infused with ***Rose Quartz Crystal and Amethyst Elixir.***

9. **PTSD FORMULA** blends special ingredients for the treatment and release of trauma and PTSD. This blend was formulated by Larry before his death to assist people who have undergone extreme trauma and are suffering from PTSD. Infused with ***Pink Calcite and Black Obsidian Elixirs.***

Genetic Oil Elixirs™

How To Order

All Genetic Oil Elixirs™ can be ordered at the Author's Website at <u>elyce@elycemonet.com</u>.

Happy Awakening and Healing with Love!

ANOINTING LOCATIONS

In Chinese Medicine, each organ contains an emotion. To understand where you need to anoint, you should be able to identify the negative stuck emotion or mental construct that needs to be cleared in the process. Here is a chart that may help you. (compliments of Gooing Chiropractic)

1) Governing Vessel (GV-20) – Brain. The Master Meridian associated with all functions of body all the way from top of the head to the bottom of the spine. Associated with cerebrospinal fluid, immune system and mental functions.

2) C1 & C2 –Brain and Central Nervous System.

   C1 - Blood Supply the Head, Bones Of The Face, Brain Inner And Middle Ear, Ears, Eyes, Pituitary Gland, Scalp, Sympathetic Nervous System

   C2 - Auditory Nerves, Eyes, Forehead, Heart, Mastoid Bones, Optic Nerves, Sinuses, Tongue Hypothalamus – Gland that links the CNS to the endocrine system via the pituitary gland. Controls the body's emotional response system.

3) Pituitary – Produces many hormones needed for the body to regulate temperature, urine, thyroid, etc.

4) Deep Sleep Point

5) Brain 2 – Emotions and Stress

6) Brain 3 – Emotions and Addictions

7) Occipital – Vision problems

8) Conception Vessel – Connected to life force (thymus). Connected to the Yin (female) meridian. Cell Energy Point

9) Kidneys – Associated with fear and cleansing of blood.

10) Pericardium – The surrounding sac of the heart. Associated with loving feelings and joy or lack of same. Links sexual energy with heart.

11) Parathyroid Glands – Associated with unexpressed anger and rage.

12) Lung – Grief and Sadness

13) Thyroid – Depression & Anxiety

14) Thymus/Heart – Links emotions with reason. Trouble can indicate an inability to balance the two.

15) Liver – Associated with anger and rage.

16) Gallbladder – Unexpressed anger that results in bitterness.

17) Stomach – Things that are indigestible

18) Pancreas – Love – Not getting enough

19) Spleen – Worry & foreboding.

20) Anterior Sacral – Negative Emotions related to Pleasure

21) Small Intestine – Digestive troubles

22) Large Intestine – Usually associated with holding on too tightly to thoughts and processes of life. Can be associated with shame and disgust. Is also connected to the Lung Meridian, where sadness and grief can be connected.

23) Bladder & Urinary Tract – The bladder is linked to social relationship conflicts, to external communication, as well as to territorial conflicts and socialization.

24) Prostate/Uterus – Feeling useless.

25) Pubic Bone – Feeling undervalued.

26) Circulation – Stagnation

27) Lymphatic – feeling a need to defend oneself, to justify oneself, in order not to feel undervalued

28) Kidney – Deep seated fear. Can be Ancestral. Fight, Fear, Shock.

29) Adrenal – Adrenal depletion is the act of not accepting what is. Fight or Flight.
30) Posterior Sacrum – Tensions associated with who I am
31) Quadriceps & Hamstrings – Fear of moving forward
32) Gluteus Maximus – Something in life is literally a pain in the butt!

Organ Meridian Acupuncture Reflex Points

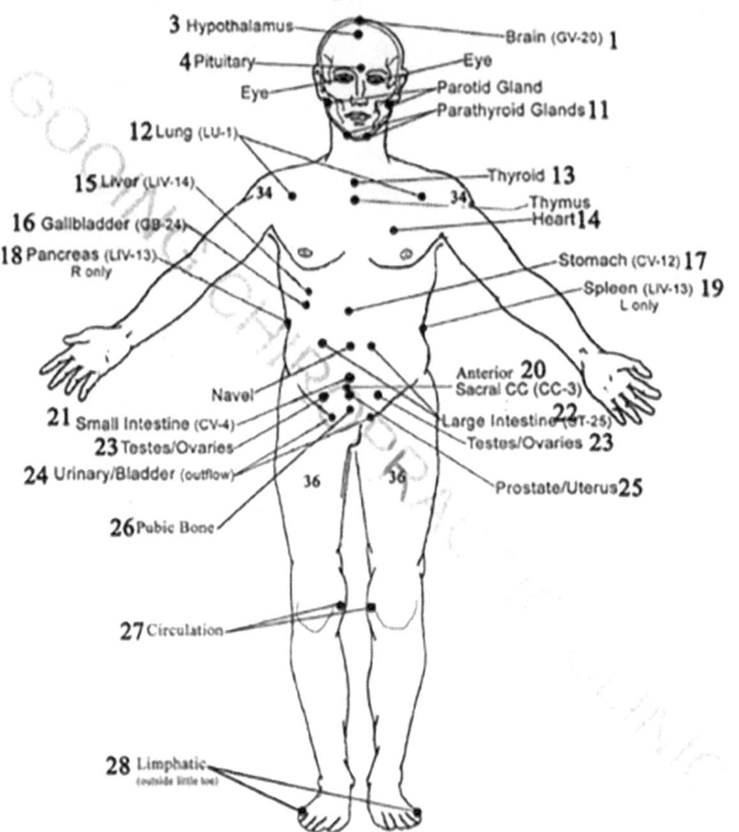

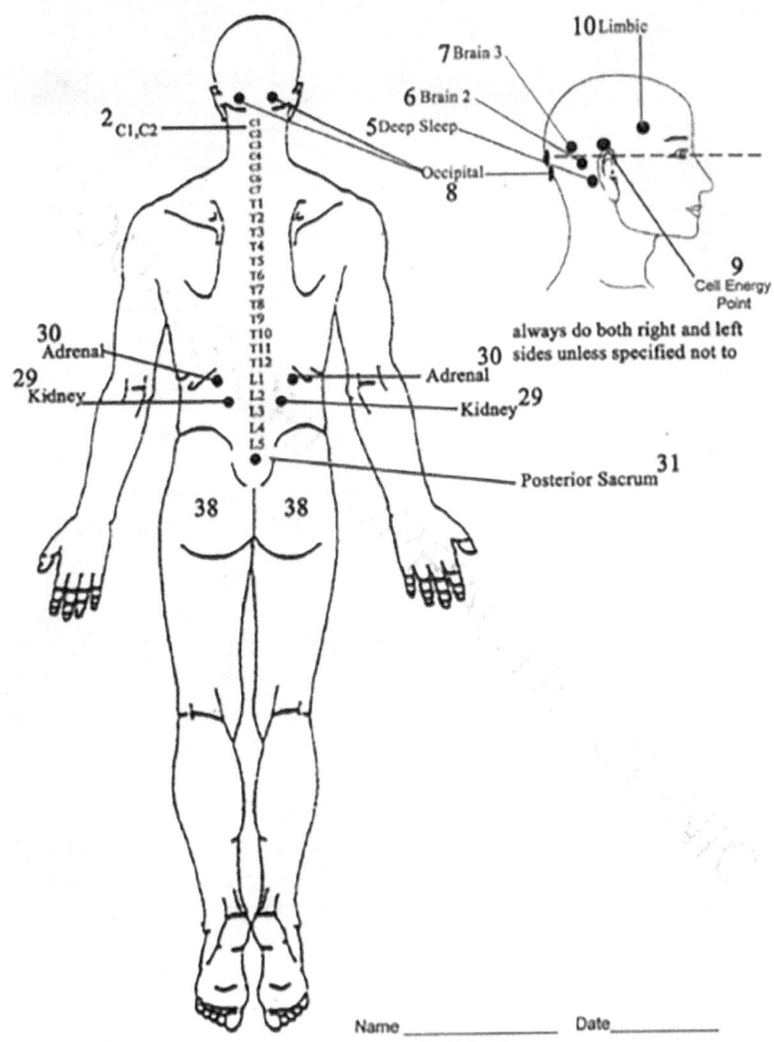
10 Limbic
7 Brain 3
6 Brain 2
5 Deep Sleep
Occipital
8
9 Cell Energy Point
2 C1,C2
C1
C2
C3
C4
C5
C6
C7
T1
T2
T3
T4
T5
T6
T7
T8
T9
T10
T11
T12
L1
L2
L3
L4
L5
30 Adrenal
29 Kidney
30 Adrenal
Kidney 29
Posterior Sacrum 31
38
38
always do both right and left sides unless specified not to
Name ______________ Date ____________

Name ____________________________________   Date _________________________________

VERTEBRAE	Areas & Parts of the Body	Possible Symtoms
BRAIN	GV20, Hypothalamus, Deep Sleep, Brain 2, Brain 3, Cell Energy, Limbic, Occipital Lobe, Parathyroid	Anxiety, Brain Fog, nervousness, insomnia, head colds, nervous breakdowns, amnesia, sleeping sickness, chronic tiredness, allergies, Immune / Auto Immune Reaction
C1	Blood supply to the head, the pituitary gland, the scalp, bones of the face, the brain itself, inner and middle ear, the sympathetic nervous system	Headaches, high blood pressure, migraine headaches, mental conditions, dizziness or vertigo, Stress Reaction, Biofilms, Heavy Metal Toxicity, Radiation Toxicity
C2	Eyes, optic nerve, auditory nerve, sinuses, mastoid bones, tongue, forehead	Sinus trouble, crossed eyes, deafness, eye troubles, earache, fainting spells, certain cases of blindness
C3	Cheeks, outer ear, face bones, teeth, trifacial nerve	Neuralgia, neuritis, acne or pimples, eczema, Neurodegeneration
C4	Nose, lips, mouth, eustachian tube	Hay fever, catarrh, hard of hearing, adenoids
C5	Vocal cords, neck glands, pharynx	Laryngitis, hoarseness, throat conditions like a sore throat or quinsy
C6	Neck muscles, shoulders, tonsils	Stiff neck, pain in upper arm, tonsillitis, whooping cough, croop
C7	Thyroid gland, bursae in the shoulders, the elbows	Bursitis, colds, thyroid conditions, goiter
T1	Arms from the elbows down, including the hands, wrists and fingers, also the esophagus and trachea	Asthma, cough, difficult breathing, shortness of breath, pain in the lower arms and hands
T2	Heart including its valves and covering, also coronary arteries	Functional heart conditions and certain chest pains
T3	Lungs, bronchial tubes, pleura, chest, breast, nipples	Bronchitis, pleurisy, pneumonia, congestion, influenza
T4	Gall bladder and common duct	Gall bladder conditions, jaundice, shingles
T5	Liver, solar plexus, blood	Liver conditions, fever, low blood pressure, anemia, poor circulation, arthritis
T6	Stomach	Stomach troubles, including nervous stomach, indigestion, heartburn, dyspepsia, etc.
T7	Pancreas, islands of Langerhans, duodenum	Diabetes, ulcers, gastritis
T8	Spleen, diaphragm	Hiccoughs, lowered resistance
T9	Adrenals or supra-renal glands	Allergies, hives
T10	Kidneys	Kidney troubles, hardening of the arteries, chronic tiredness, nephritis, pyelitis
T11	Kidneys, ureters	Skin conditions like acne, pimples, eczema, or boils
T12	Small intestines, fallopian tubes	Rheumatism, gas pains, certain types of sterility
L1	Large intestines or colon, inguinal rings	Constipation, colitis, dysentery, diarrhea, ruptures or hernias
L2	Appendix, abdomen, upper leg, cecum	Appendicitis, cramps, difficult breathing, acidosis, varicose veins
L3	Sex organs, ovaries or testicles, uterus, bladder, knee, circulation	Bladder troubles, menstrual troubles like painful or irregular periods, miscarriages, bed wetting, impotency, change of life symptoms, many knee pains
L4	Prostate gland, muscles of the lower back, sciatic nerve	Sciatica, lumbago, difficult, painful, or too frequent urination, backache
L5	Lower legs, ankles, feet, toes, arches, lymph	Poor circulation in the legs, swollen ankles, weak ankles and arches, cool feet, weakness in the legs, leg cramps
SACRUM	Hip Bones, buttocks, Pubic Bone	Sacro-Ialic conditions, spinal curvatures
COCCYX	Rectum, anus	Hemorrhoids or piles, pruritis or itching, pain at the end of spine on sitting

GOOING CHIROPRACTIC CLINIC (714) 556-9188 www.drgooing.com

SACRED PRAYERS

The prayers here are designed to assist you in going into your own heart. They are written from my heart and stated as I would be talking directly to Creator. The best kinds of prayers are those from your own heart! They are real. Creator isn't concerned with the words you use. He is concerned with your state of being (heart). The sample prayers simply give you a way to know how to pray.

<u>General Healing Prayer (Truth)</u>

Suggested Oils: Holy Anointing Oils Forehead between
the Eyes (Third Eye) Palms and Bottoms of Feet

Father in Heaven and within my heart, lean in to hear my request.

Archangels, Enlightened Masters and Ancestral Guides of Light, draw near, hear me, protect me, and comfort me.

I have fallen short, yet know that all things can be made pure and whole.

Restore me to my original Divine Blueprint without stain or mark.

Feed my soul with pure manna from Heaven, your Divine Love and sustenance.

Restore me to my Higher Self.

Clear me of my injustices, my fear and negative emotions, and guide and direct my path.

My body is giving way to my own negative choices in life. I am guilty of

_________________________.

Show me the truth of my crooked road. Show me a better way. Fill me with healing light and love.

Heal me now I pray, in Jesus Name.

<u>Self-Forgiveness (Grace)</u>

Suggested Oils: Oil of The Magdalene,
Anointing Oils, Three Kings
Palms, Third Eye, Bottoms of Feet, Kidneys

Mother/Father Creator, I need your tender mercy and strength. My limbs are numb from my own mistakes. My soul is weary.

Create in me a clean heart. Help me to lean on you rather than stay in my mind and its worldly games of power and control.

Connect me to my higher awareness, and let me feel deeply the pain I have inflicted on myself and on others. I am aware of it. I acknowledge what I have created.

I am ready to change my ways. I am ready to consider others as being connected with me. What I do to my brother or sister, I do to myself. Forgive me also for not responding when you tried to show me truth. Forgive me for becoming stiff necked at your lessons.
Heal me from my pride.
Heal me from my anger.
Heal me from my fear.

If you are with me, no one can be against me.

I trust in the Lord with all my heart, and forsake the way of the world. Show me the way.

Abba, Father. Amma, Mother.

Let me heal from my mind, will and emotions. Let me feel whole in your presence and love.

<u>**Forgiveness of Others (Surrender)**</u>

Suggested Oils: Rose of Sharon, Three Kings,
Gold, Frankincense & Myrrh
Palms, Third Eye, Bottoms of Feet, Tops of Feet, Throat, Heart

Heavenly Father/Mother,

My heart is broken within me. I am carrying anger/bitterness/ resentment for my spouse/brother/sister/friend/coworker/child.

They have caused me great pain and I can't let it go. What is it within me that created this? Help me to see.

What is it within them that wanted this situation? Help me to understand.

Help me to accept all responsibility for my part. Help me to forgive them for their part, in the same measure as I forgive myself.

Set me on the wings of the Eagle, so that I may soar above the circumstances of this situation. Let me fly high with a new perspective through your eyes.

Let me clear my body, mind, and heart of all desire to return the pain and suffering.

Help me to see he/she who has hurt me as something within me that needed to be addressed.

Let me clear myself, and leave their choices between them and You.

Help me to truly forgive, and let go of all retribution, anxiety, worry and sorrow.

Betrayal (Courage)

Suggested Oils: Oils of Courage and Three Kings Back of Neck,
Third Eye, Behind Knees, Palms, Bottom of Feet, Kidneys, Heart

Mother/Father Creator, I am at my lowest point.

Please surround me with protection from my Angels, Guides and Masters who are working with me.

Those whom I trusted have betrayed me. It feels like they were never my friend, yet I know we are connected for a reason.

Help me to perceive this betrayal as a needed lesson from you. Help me not to lash out in anger and return pain for pain.

Help me to let go of all the anger and rage and resentment I feel now. I know if it will stick in my body and keep me sick if I hang on to it, but I don't know how to let it go.

So, I confess that I can't do it by myself. Help me, O Lord, to release the pain. Help me to trust in you.

Help me to believe that you are my rear guard, and I have nothing to fear.

My limbs are weak and my heart barely beats.

Thank you for this lesson. Help me to understand it in the days to come. Help me to forgive my brother/sister so that I can move forward in love.

Give me strength and peace in my hour of need.

<u>Negative Emotions (Hopelessness, Anger, Fear, Rage, Intolerance, Pride, Selfishness)</u>

Suggested Oils: Oils of Courage, Oils of
the Magdalene, Three Kings
Third Eye, Back of Neck, Ears, Kidneys, Palms, Bottoms of Feet

Divine Mother,

I am drowning in my own emotions. Save me! Help me to let go of projecting my negative emotions on others. Help me to release the negative energy within me so that I can me clear and focused on love.

Create in me a clean heart, as you bring awareness of the thoughts that are creating these emotions within me.

Are they ancestral patterns? If so, let me heal from the transgressions of my lineage.

Are they my own creation in habits and patterns? If so, show me where I am blind to what I am doing.

Restore to me the righteousness of Creator. I AM HOLY. Let me feel HOLY. Raise my vibration to a state of joy. Help me to let go of my judgments and preconceptions of my own reality.

Help me to breathe deeply and receive the Holy Spirit through breath.

Let all negative entities and dark spirits be cast out of my body and field. Help me to understand where to go to get help if they are controlling me.

Create in me a clean heart.

<u>Physical Illness (Disease)</u>

Suggested Oils: Holy Anointing Oil on 3rd crown; Three Kings on 3rd Eye; Oils of Courage on neck and spine; Rose of Sharon on Brain 2 & 3; Oil of Solomon on navel and coccyx; Oil of the Magdalene on palms and soles of feet. You can also place any of these oils on specific organs that need healing.

Father/Mother Creator,

I am suffering in my physical body. I call in the Angels, Guides & Masters to create a double diamond tetrahedron of white light around me with mirrors facing inward to magnify and intensify my healing. I pray that they will bring forth illumination of my mind to understand the reason I am ill.

I ask for understanding for the cause of my dis-ease and its remedy. Why am I sick? Is it unto death?

Am I glorifying you as I undergo this trauma? Create in me the desire to manifest good health.

Create in me the ability to utilize the elements of air, fire, water, earth and ethers to alchemize whatever needs to be re-created in my life.

Show me the negative emotions that created this dis-ease.
Show me the mental belief systems that need to be changed.

Free me from the bonds of my own emotional/psychological prison. Free me from the belief that I need something physical to heal me. All I need is YOU.

Restoring Balance (As Above, So Below;
As Within, So Without)

Suggested Oils: Oil of Gladness on Brain 2 and Brain 3; Rose of Sharon on throat; Gold, Frankincense & Myrrh on crown and feet; Holy Anointing Oil on 3rd Eye; Oils of Courage on Solar Plexus and Kidneys

Father/Mother Creator,

I see where my life is out of balance.

I see where I am leading with my (masculine) (feminine) side and have neglected balance in my life.

I want to balance my life.

I want to honor my relationships so that all people feel loved and cherished by me.

I want to balance my time so that my values are in alignment with what is truly important.

Help me to understand who I have been being, and where I need to change.

Help to have the courage to consciously choose a new way of aligning my values and balancing my life.

Help me to consider my loved ones most important.

Create in me a clean and balanced life.

<u>Addiction (Self Control)</u>

Suggested Oils: Holy Anointing Oil on Crown and
3rd Eye; Rose of Sharon on Heart; Oil of Solomon on
throat and solar plexus; Oils of Courage on back of
heart and temples; Three Kings on palms and feet

Father Creator,

I call in the Archangels and Masters of Light who work with me. I am aware that I am helpless in my addiction.

I know that you have the power to heal all things, and that it is me who keeps falling into old habits and patterns of escapism.

My heart is wounded. My thoughts are impure.

Create in me the will to create a clean and holy life.

Create in me the ability to see myself as I truly am…. Loved, connected and accepted just as I AM.

Help me to feel the truth of who I AM. Create in me a clean heart.

Bind in me all forces who are working against my healing

Remove from my life all people who take me down and tempt me.

You always provide an escape. Give me that escape now in dramatic ways. I love you, Lord Creator. In you I place my trust. Help me to bend to your will.

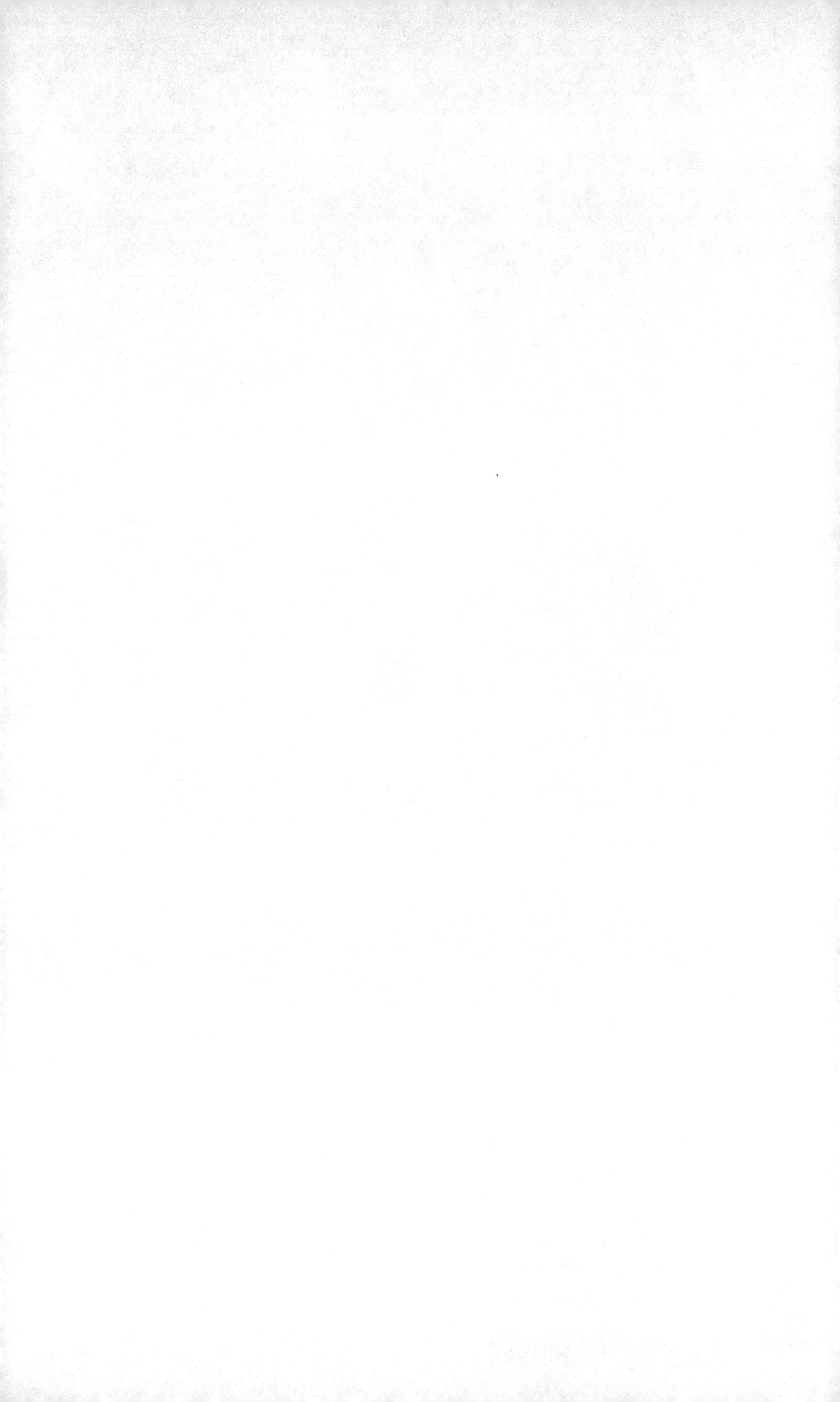

www.ingramcontent.com/pod-product-compliance
Lightning Source LLC
Chambersburg PA
CBHW031033190726
48286CB00003BA/1146